Distinguished member of the international society of poets. Twice winner of the outstanding literary achievement award and also a bronze medallist. Every poem submitted has been published and one has been broadcast. My aim is to keep young minds open to other than the immediate.

Anne - for encouragement and endless cups of tea.

Gideon Lambert

TIKKA

AUSTIN MACAULEY PUBLISHERS™

LONDON • CAMBRIDGE • NEW YORK • SHARJAH

A CIP catalogue record for this title is available from the British Library.

ISBN 9781398478848 (Paperback)
ISBN 9781398478855 (ePub e-book)

www.austinmacauley.com

First Published 2023
Austin Macauley Publishers Ltd®
1 Canada Square
Canary Wharf
London
E14 5AA

To my publishers for their kindness and patience.

Chapter One

I'm clocking on a bit now, kids. Retired and living in the big city – the one they call 'The Smoke'. All right, no need to bother your parents. London, I meant.

I thought – time to 'fess up. About Tikka, that is. You may not believe a word.

Still, it makes a good tale, so here goes.

Believe it or not I was young once. Not so long ago! Well, admittedly in the last century – just over the halfway mark. No computers as we know them now. Nor cell phones, yes there was such a time!

I grew up in a small village next to an extensive area of moorland in the south-west of our glorious nation. I won't say exactly where. I don't want to start a sudden tourist invasion! Where was I? Oh yes, the Moor. I adored every heathery acre. I could reel off the names of all the species of flora and fauna, you know – animals and plants. So could Super-Sal, my fellow villager and classmate at the secondary modern school in town. Fellow naturalists, we cycled together at weekends and sometimes during holiday breaks, as nature buffs I know not how we fell for Scruffy Hollershaw's rare bird wind-up. Fall we did!

Summer term! Well-named, Scruffy approached us both one Friday lunchtime. He informed his two gullible classmates that rare birds had been sighted in a disused quarry some miles distant.

"What kinda birds?" I was suspicious.

"Beefeaters, I fink."

Sal chortled. "Beefeaters wear fancy hats and guard the Tower of London. You mean bee eaters, dopey."

"I'm no horni – horni – thologist, am I? It was in The Mercury. All those twitchy types having a butchers (look)."

We were in no position to argue. My selfish dad always spirited away the local rag (newspaper) immediately the paper boy lobbed it onto the step. To Mum's annoyance, he always forgot where he put it. Super-Sal's parents never took the thing so …

We took Scruffy on trust. Alas, trust proved in short supply around him. Yet, in an odd way, I owe him. Without his twisted take on life, I would likely never have met Tikka!

Next morning Sal and I, armed with cameras and notebooks, set off. Scruffy was no doubt chortling to himself somewhere.

A part of the journey crossed the moor. We had to pass 'The Great Mire'. We always kept clear due to local rumours of foxes, ponies and even humans being sucked down into it. Dad insisted that was just local 'eyewash'.

Level with the Great Mire, I slammed my foot into the springy heather. Sal halted just ahead of me.

"What now?" Her saddle was going wonky and we had neglected to bring a screwdriver. She was bad company.

I pointed. "Dog! No owner."

You need your specs, Four-eyes. Mound of earth, that's all.

I was sensitive about my NHS specs – close vision only Wish that was still … Anyways, I knew what I was seeing.

A ginormous canine, hairy but with a greyhoundy head. He was stretched out on a grassy mound with his elongated muzzle resting on his bulging forepaws. Only his eyes, large and liquidy, betrayed that he was alert. They swivelled between Sal and me, noting every move.

"It's you needing specs, Sal. Right on top of the mound, and it's mostly rock, that mound. Well, earthy rock with grass on top – oh, and the dog of course."

"Yeah right. Noah's Ark's next door. Wondered where it landed."

In unison we exclaimed, "You are just winding me up!"

"We can't just leave him here, Sal. Supposing he wanders into the mire?"

"Funnee! Come on, Doopy-Dopey. Mum wants me back by teatime."

"Mine too, but …"

"'Nuff. Let's roll." Sal was a fan of a new cowboy television show called 'Wagon Train'.

The dog was still studying us. *Maybe the fact that I looked his way so anxiously clicked with him. Who knows?*

Ruddy good acting by Sal pretending she couldn't see him. In our school play, as third Roman citizen in hessian robe, she had managed to screw up the word 'rhubarb'.

No twitchers. No bee eaters. We had been ... well, had! Just a deserted quarry – and us!

We consumed our packed lunches. I kept back part of a roast beef sandwich filling in case we encountered that giant hound on the return journey.

We didn't. Just two morose, would-be Gerald Durrells cycling homeward in the dusk. Both of us were nursing vengeful thoughts regarding Scruffy Hollershaw.

I was lead cyclist for once. Normally Sal was, but that skewed saddle was taking its toll. She described her symptoms as 'gross chafing in the nether region'.

"Sounds like the name of a village." I smirked.

She was not amused. I maintained a tactful silence in order to survive the remainder of the journey. Sal packed a mean right hook, courtesy of her boxing uncle.

As to Scruffy – time to check his passport. Doubt if he had one!

Chapter Two

Church day! My merciful parents granted me a reprieve. A vote of sympathy after yesterday's fruitless quest ending in a deserted quarry resembling a film set moonscape.

I lay in my ground floor bedroom, smugly listening to my parents preparing themselves for their weekly endurance test. Reverend Boomer's sermons lived up to his name. Even adults found them a poor alternative to watching paint dry.

While breakfast crockery clattered and clinked in the next room – the kitchen – my sleepy mind was picturing Scruffy being marched across the playground in his notoriously baggy underpants by yours truly. Revenge can be very sweet! Suddenly, I had a weird sense of being watched.

My bedroom curtains did not hang right. They only closed with the aid of a bulldog clip. In summer, I usually left them apart sufficiently to admit fresh air from the open window. Oh, and any rays of sunlight able to slant across my face.

Something was obstructing the usual sunbeams. My misted vision swivelled to take in a long muzzle and a pair of curious canine eyes through the V-shaped curtain gap. The eyes were studying me!

I barely blinked. Image gone. Imagination? No!

I willed my parents' departure to be quick. Untypically they obliged. Car engine idling in the drive, clump of Mum's 'sensible' shoes, slam of car doors, vehicle's gentle purr fading into distance. Me – alone at last.

If there was a dog around, thank goodness my anti-pooch dad had not encountered it. I needed to find it big-time!

To have peered into my bedroom – this monster canine must have rested both forepaws on my outside windowsill. I was much more concerned that the huge hind feet would have been 'planted' firmly in Mum's beloved herbaceous border.

I dressed and raced to that spot. Not a single crushed herb. To my utter bewilderment not a single indentation in the soft, loose soil. The pressure of that immense bulk ought to have created deep soil prints.

"Holy Jupiter," I exclaimed. My strict Methodist Gran would have been outraged at my verbal outburst.

Finally, I decided I had been dreaming after seeing that giant hound out on the moor. Yes, that was it – a dream.

I was wrong – totally wrong!

Chapter Three

I had always wanted a dog. Well, it's every kid's right to own one, isn't it?

Even Super-Sal had Snooks, the terrier. No dream dog, Snooksie. Only active in pursuit of the tabby next door. One mean moggy that gave him quite a pasting when cornered.

Hardly a dream dog, but a dog nevertheless. Love is blind and Snooksie was the apple of Sal's eyeball.

For me, no dog. The 'hobstacle', to quote our then-village bobby, was my dad. I didn't blame him. As a kid (centuries before), he was mauled in the street by a half-starved German shepherd. Boy, I hear you say. No wonder he was turning cannibal, that shepherd, if his sheep had wandered so far. No, it's not a person. German shepherd is the old name for an Alsatian dog.

Despite the efforts of the medics at the local cottage hospital, Dad was left with a permanent zig-zag scar on his left forearm. Self-conscious about it, he never wore short-sleeved shirts. Nor did he ever roll up his sleeves at the timber merchants where he worked. Worse, from my viewpoint, he had grown up with 'doggy phobia'. If he was at home when Lassie or Rin Tin Tin (my two favourite TV stars) were on, he never got emotionally involved. Mum and I wept for Lassie's failing eyesight and thanked God for that conveniently tender-hearted eye surgeon. I sat on the edge of my chair when 'Rinty' was captured by redskins. Dad, on both occasions, simply left the room.

So, no dog! Just a sombre guinea pig called Morton, a consolation present resulting from Dad's guilt trip over the matter. Fond of Morton as I was, I could hardly trail him behind me on cycle outings. Even reaching his cage water-bottle was a major expedition. During games of cops and robbers, popular even amongst older kids in those more innocent times … well, what kind of criminal mastermind would recoil in terror from a police guinea pig?

"Go get him, Morton," had a hollow ring to it.

With far less homework then, I was free to cycle around the edge of the moor in the dusk. Post-supper, I assumed the role of a patrolling roundhead officer based on imagination and school history lessons. I doubt that many roundhead officers had strict instructions to be indoors by 7:45 pm. Also, my bike was a poor stand-in for a roundhead pony.

A couple of evenings later, as I turned my bike homeward, a bat skimmed my head and disappeared into nearby gardens. Straining to follow its progress in the dusk, I almost collided – or so it seemed – with none other than that hairy super hound from the moor. I was nearly catapulted over the bike handlebars.

He seemed totally unmoved by the incident, unlike me. He simply stood there with his active tail punishing the ground beneath him.

A dog is a dog, is a dog, is a dog. Especially to a dog-deprived schoolboy. Moreover, once again – no sign of an owner. However, as I dismounted, he backed off. This was his first sign of alarm.

"OK feller. I won't hurt you."

Too true. By his size, one gulp would have rendered me yesterday's news. Still, he was the nervous one.

After a few failed attempts to get up close and personal, I watched in dismay as he loped off across the darkening moor.

"Boy, I screwed up big time there." My dialogue then was based on Lassie's TV owner, played by one Tommy Rettig, a catarrhal youngster smothered with affection by his overzealous mom and grandpa (known as 'Gramps').

I did 'screw up', but not 'bigtime'. To his delighted surprise, the would-be roundhead found the dog waiting for him at the nearest crossroads the very following evening! On subsequent evenings, too. Even at weekends, forcing me to make major timetable and general routine adjustments.

Off we would go onto the near edge of the moor. Ahead of me he seemed to flow rather than run with an easy grace that was unlike any dog I had seen before. Or any dog I have seen since!

In case you are wondering how I knew I was dealing with a male dog, not a female – well, he was running in front of me. Get your blushing parents to explain that one. I absolve myself of all responsibility!

I never tried to close in on him again. I was just too scared he might disappear on me for good.

One curious thing among many – he never barked. At least, he never made any vocal sound in my presence.

To my relief, he always left me on our return to that crossroads. He simply turned and loped off towards the moor. Not even a backward glance! A mystery dog. But what did I care. I had my very own pooch for a short period every day. And what a pooch. He made Snooksie look like Morton!

Chapter Four

B oy." Everything was boy. Boy this, boy that. Not that he took any notice. He simply led the way or ran round my bike in wide, lazy circles.

Time to give him a name. Selfish me! His actual owner might already have named him. Still, he responded well to – Tikka. Nothing to do with a now popular Asian food dish. At that period, I would never have heard of it. No! On Dad's personal bookshelf were two hardcover children's books. They dated from his childhood. I found them … magnetic. I was constantly delving into them. 'Tarka the Otter' and the anthologised 'Jungle Book'. The latter one by the now less popular author I jokingly called Kipyard Rudling contained a story about a rare mongoose named Rikki Tikki Tavi.

'Tarka' and 'Tikki' united in my mind to give me 'Tikka'. So Tikka, my mystery dog, became! Why mystery? Well, he was just that – mysterious. Assuming I did not dream up his brief Sunday visit to my home as I first thought – then how did he know where I lived? Did he shadow me homeward from that Saturday forlorn bee-eater foray? If he did, I suggest that any private eye would pay big bucks to know his secret!

Also, how did he evade my eye line on the moor. Moors are flat or flatfish, mainly below the natural tree line. What was he – a ninja dog (not that I knew that word then).

Who was the owner? There was less traffic on the roads than now, but fancy letting him wander about unsupervised.

I told you I would not risk approaching him. Instead, I elected to lure him close to me. The bait was to be basic proprietary dog food. True, he looked very well-fed already, but I was counting on greed, not need.

Three tins of 'Bonso' dog-mix – jumbo size – from the village store set my pocket money back by two shillings and sixpence. You know – half a crown. No? Oh, don't let's go there!

Gangly Reuben appeared as if by magic one evening at the crossroads as I spread the food on a piece of cardboard. 'Reub', as we called him, was a local farmhand. The first human, apart from Sal, to be around when I was with Tikka.

"Blimey! You must be hungry, mate!" Reuben was uni-material. It would not have taken him five minutes to get a degree in sarcasm. That is why my pretty cousin Becky dumped him.

"I'm feeding the dog." I nodded towards Tikka who sat further along the grass roadside verge, all swivel-eyed with curiosity.

"Yeah mate. Right. What are you on? Better not be feedin' them foxes. If they gets near the gaffer's henhouse an' he finds out you're encouragin' 'em, you're for it!"

Off he went whistling tunelessly. I knew he wouldn't 'split' on me. Apart from a recall that would shame a goldfish, he was indifferent to everything but girls. Girls, girls, girls. That was Reub – but what was all that foxy blether?

Nothing could outstrip the total indifference my monster-dog exhibited towards his doggy-fest. But I was not noticing that any more.

Revelation! The truth had finally exploded in my brain. The Berlin Wall had crumbled early.

Reub had perfect eyesight in spite of a slight squint. 20/20 vision! Yet, following my gaze towards Tikka, he had seen nothing! Hence all the foxy gibberish.

My mind revolved back to that first sighting of Tikka on the moor. Sighting for me – yes, but not Sal! Far from winding me up, she had not been able to see him at all.

Either I was several links short of an anchor chain or Tikka was invisible to everyone but me. I had some kind of ghost dog? A spook? What old Mr Pargeter would have called 'a fissic phenomenon'.

Chapter Five

Who was old Mr Pargeter? I'll tell you. A near-neighbour beloved of all the village kids.

An ancient man with a wonky eye permanently shadowed by the peak of his flat cap. His favourite 'summer perch', as he termed it, was the decaying trunk of a long since fallen oak tree just beyond his own cottage back garden. Like a king holding court – only all his subjects were children.

Any youngster that stopped to listen would be regaled with stories and legends as well as true local history. He knew about smugglers and river pirates, haunted dells, the moor itself. He spoke with gentle authority and enlivened his chat with humour aimed at the young. His jokes always hit their target with us kids – a knack denied to most adults.

I have witnessed him spellbinding an audience of 'young uns' as he called them. Some on the log with him, others sprawled on the grass, plunging grimy fingers into the open bag of mint humbugs he left near his slippered feet.

I needed to confide in some adult about Tikka. I knew he would not scoff. His mind was as open as one of his humbug bags.

One bright Saturday morning I sought him out. Mum and Dad were in town shopping, Sal was visiting a distant relative with her parents. So time was in plentiful supply.

I found him sitting on his log. He was attempting to read a copy of 'The Mercury'. His specs were balanced precariously on account of them having only one arm. He was mouthing the words to himself.

He set the paper aside and removed the specs. He was plainly relieved to be interrupted in such a delicate balancing act. It was good to find him alone. As good as it was rare!

"Well, well. Long-time no see. How are yer, boy?"

"Fine thanks, Mr P. I do need to talk to you."

"You are doing. Have a mint humbug."

"Ta. It's about my dog."

"Easy settled. You don't have one."

"Do."

"It must be in the Secret Service."

I poured out the story. For once, he did all the listening. But, like the great old guy he was, he did not scoff. Not so much as a chortle! His rugged old face stayed composed and serious.

There was a short pause before he eventually responded. There always was. "I think I may have a clue as to what your doggy friend is all about, boy. Now, let's find out if I have it with me."

He fumbled in the deep side-pocket of his long, dusty coat. I was left to boggle at what 'it' might be.

'It' finally came forth, in company with several Rizla cigarette papers and a plug of tobacco. A small – almost tiny – carving in unstained wood. Very rough and ready, as though somebody had been whittling with a slightly blunted knife or blade.

My jaw dropped. Basic and crude as it was, it depicted the rough outline of a man clutching a sort of spear. But my attention was directed to the base of the carving. Where it flared out slightly was a dog shape with an extended muzzle and a greyhoundy head. Various nicks in the wood suggested a shaggy pelt. It was all so reminiscent of Tikka! Wow!!

"Should have passed this ancient feller to the town museum yonks ago. Found it out on the moor when I was a young man. Yeah, there was such a time."

"That dog looks like …"

"I reckoned so when I heard your little tale. And it all connects with a legend. Did I ever tell you about the hunter and his dog?"

"Don't fink so."

"No fs in think. You are right, though. I didn't. Glaring omission."

"You did tell me about that visit to the moor by that famous highwayman – er – Dick Turpin."

"Don't let me off the hook, boy. Glaring omission."

He patted the tree trunk. "Park yourself. Time to rectify things. Remember legends are not necessarily fact, but truth like this little carving has many grains."

I looked at him vaguely. "I'm all ears, Mr P."

"That's 'cus your fond mama never laid you on your side as a baby. Have another mint humbug before I launch."

"Ta."

"There was this hunter, see. Mighty like Nimrod – or was it Nimrud?"

"Who?"

"And you from a church-going family. Read your Bible. Book of Genesis. Good for your soul. Now, I would like to finish this story before Armageddon. No, don't ask."

"I won't speak again."

"Where was I? Oh, mighty hunter. It may have been in Saxon times or even earlier. Plenty of forest about then, so I expect he used to hunt boar and deer – even wolves and that. He was built like a brick khasi so, boy, could he hunt."

"A what?"

"Never mind. Let's just say he looked like Marvel man in those comics I have seen you reading. Mind, he was dressed in furs, not all that skin-tight clobber."

"Wow!"

"Shhh. Anyhow, he lived up-country aways. But once he did come down to this moor of ours."

"Why?"

"I dunno everything, do I? Happen his old mum moved house and he was visiting. Not important, matey. What matters is that he bumped into this voluptuous maiden – the daughter of a local settlement headman."

"Volupchus. Cor!"

"Here, at your tender age you are not to be 'coring' at such things. For somebody who was not going to utter, you stand badly in need of a mouth-cosy. Anyhow, they fell in love – the huntsman and the maiden. They obtained Daddy's permission to get spliced. Wed!

"The wedding was to take place a few days later at midnight, preferably under a full moon, as was the custom then. However, it was also the custom for the huntsman to bring his ceremonial spear to the wedding. He had to return to his settlement beyond the Great Forest the other side of the moor to fetch the spear.

"Before departing, he took advice on the best return route. Only he took it from a black-hearted local official who also burned with passion for the voluptuous maiden."

"Cor!"

"I warned you. No coring. Anyhow, the official played on the huntsman's superstitions and persuaded him to come back on the wedding night itself before the midnight hour – but only just. He convinced him if he even glimpsed the bride before the ceremony, the marriage would be doomed. Cursed!

"The huntsman had only ever crossed the moor by daylight. The official's false directions ensured that by night he would enter the Great Mire. It was swampier then on account of the heavier rainfall.

"On the wedding night the hunter emerged from his beloved forest onto the alien moor. With him was his faithful hunting dog."

"Tikka?"

"Possibly. Anyhow, no doubt Mr Moon was hovering in readiness to shine on the nuptials."

"What chills?"

"On the wedding and the feast to follow. Keep up!

"Suddenly Mr Moon found himself masked by a huge, dark cloud courtesy of that jealous official who was rumoured to have some skill in the black arts. Never mind asking what they are. Not proper for you to know yet.

"Much of what followed is – and was – pure guesswork. But although the hunter and his dog were alone it all comes under what we call now reasonable supposition. A good guess!

"In the pitch darkness the hunter blundered into the swampy mire and began to sink. He flung his ceremonial spear onto solid ground so others might find it and guess his fate. Then his faithful hound …"

"Tikka?"

"His faithful hound extended its long muzzle across the swamp and reached the hunter's furry collar. It strained to pull him free. But he was a feller built to last. Rather than the dog pulling him free, his huge bulk was dragging the animal down.

"At the last the hunter, resigned to his own fate, somehow seized that huge doggy. He flung him back onto solid ground. A lump of fur was still tangled round the dog's fangs. Meanwhile the hunter's head and neck were vanishing into the mud."

"Where was the rest of him?"

"Did your mum put your cap on straight when you used to go to the village primary school? I seem to remember it was crooked – like your thinking. The rest of him was already down under the mud. I said earlier he began to sink but he wasn't doing handstands at the time.

"Anyway, when the hunter did not show, the headman thundered; 'Nobody jilts my daughter' – or words to that effect."

"Jilts?"

"Leaves at the altar, so to speak. The sorrowful maiden was thinking clearer than Pa. She knew the strength of the hunter's love for her was equal to hers for him. She demanded that the headman take a search party out on the moor next morning.

"As that party approached the Great Mire, they heard an ear-splitting howl like a soul in torment. They were able to enter the mire 'cus the headman himself knew every stick, stone and blade of grass."

"And all them boggy bits."

"Who is telling this tale? Beside one very boggy bit, they found the faithful hound with both forepaws across the hunter's ceremonial spear. The hunter's fate was obvious.

"As they drew near, the dog snarled, showing the fur material round his choppers. Sorry, fangs to you! He showed no sign of surrendering that spear – the last link with his master.

"Though they incurred fearful injuries these strong warriors somehow overpowered the great hound. Securing his long muzzle with leather straps, they set him on a crude sled and conveyed him back to the settlement.

"When she heard what had likely befallen the hunter, the grief-stricken bride-to-have-been sought the evil official. She had glimpsed him talking to the hunter when giving him false directions so she had a good notion of what he had done!

"He made the big mistake of declaring his passion for her, confirming her suspicions. Motive, you see!

"Her grief gave way to blinding fury. She seized a wooden pointed stake nearby and plunged it into the man so deep it all but came out the other side. Blood everywhere I expect."

"Ugh! Like ketchup. Did the cops come and nick her?"

"This was before police as we know them. Rough justice in more primitive times. There was no sympathy for him."

"And Tikka?"

"The maiden was quite some gal, despite her hot temper. Brave as a lioness defending her cubs, she was. She unstrapped that monster hound. No doubt her Pa and his followers stood round them both with poised spears. No need 'cus that dog must have sensed her link with his master. The legend records that he even wagged • his tail feebly when she stroked him."

"Cor. She was brave!"

"She was. He stayed with her for some weeks. But he never forgot his beloved master.

"Daily he entered that swampy mire alone. Locals glimpsed him crouching where the headman had plunged the hunter's spear tip-first into the earth. As a marker of where the hunter went down. Glimpsed and heard 'cus that dog howled regular. Just like a wolf howls at the moon, only more tormented."

"Poor, poor Tikka. Did the maiden become a nun, like in films and that?"

"Nope. Police and nuns came about a deal later I suspect. The legend starts to peter out at this point. Some authorities say she never truly recovered from her grief and loss and she took her own life."

"Authorities?"

"Experts past and present. Don't you want to know what became of the hunter's dog – curious boy?"

"I was scared to ask."

"It is said that both the headman's daughter and the dog plunged into the swamp together, right where the spear marked the fate of the young hunter."

"Who says?"

"Something called folk memory or tradition. But the legend is very old and there are other versions of it. They tell us that the maiden died alone and the hound wandered away to die of a broken heart. What we call pining. I believe the first version."

"Why?"

"So dramatic. Makes a better story ending. Only a legend, mind, but it might explain your ghost-doggy if that is what he is."

Chapter Six
Summer Holidays at Last!

In those post-war days us kids were swept off to 'exotic seaside resorts with strange-sounding names' (to quote an old ballad song). It makes one quite heady to reel off the main list: Weston-Super-Mare, Brighton, Eastbourne, Whitstable, Margate and Herne Bay. For the more upmarket families with the elevated noses, there was glorious Bournemouth!

Sal's parents, drunk with the spirit of adventure this year, elected for the Isle of Wight. Taking the ferry to that 'far-off foreign clime' was considered hard-core tourism then. Would they ever make it back?

Fearless Freddy – my only other classmate who was also a fellow villager – went down with measles. No sorry – German measles – the one his father, an ex-wartime paratrooper, swore blind was the Huns' revenge for defeat in two successive world wars. One way or another, Freddy was quarantined. Out of action. Shame! I liked to kick a football around with him.

You see, I also was going nowhere. Dad was caught up in some emergency at the timber yard. Mum, on the other hand, was caught up with Aunt Millie. She was Mum's only sister. She relieved what I now realise must have been a dreary spinster's existence in town by collecting illnesses to suffer from. They usually came along in roughly alphabetical order, those maladies based on her copy of a well-known medical encyclopaedia. Despite constant reassurances from her unfortunate GPs, she was very determined to consider herself permanently at death's door.

As I travelled homeward on the school bus from town to village, my frequent glimpses of Aunt Millie racing to the nearby Scout Hall cast doubt on her ailing conditions. The lure of 'housey-housey' (a form of bingo) certainly effected daily temporary miracle cures. She would be moving so fast it was a wonder her feet did not spark.

Mum, under Dad's stony gaze, usually managed to wriggle out of going to stay with the so-called invalid. Not this time! A young and raw new GP had personally phoned and appealed to Mum to come over and monitor Aunt Millie, who had an apparent fever.

With Mum absent from nine to seven every day, I was left to my own devices. I converted my meals of meat and salad left in the fridge for me into packed lunches. Well, sort of!

Taking advantage of the glorious weather, I went cycling alone on my beloved moor. In my heart, I almost blessed Aunt Millie!

Also, I had been worried about holidaying because it would prevent me rendezvousing with Tikka each evening. Now that anxiety was lifted. So I thought! But to my dismay, for the first couple of evenings of the holiday, he failed to turn up at the crossroads.

However, on the third morning (after two sleepless nights) I happened to be cycling near the Great Mire. There he was as I first encountered him. Crouching on that very same mound, I think. At sight of me he stood majestically and extended to his full body length. His bushy tail gave the heather and its insect occupants something to think about. He was pleased to see me, but it was almost like he expected me. Strange!

As I cycled on, he suddenly overtook me to race ahead. I pressed resolutely on but was aware that he kept glancing back towards the mire over his powerful shoulders. Gradually I secured his compliance with the direction I took, but he seemed reluctant to let the mire vanish from view. Even though he was taking the lead I could sense the tension in him every time he turned his head towards it.

Suddenly we came upon a moorland pony herd. I don't know how aware those animals were of my ghost dog. Their skittishness might have been just due to the enchanting baby foal in their midst, needing protection.

Tikka surveyed the herd and me distantly. His gaze was mournful yet detached as I hunkered down on the grass. He maintained this air of quiet sadness while I came to grips with my misshapen doorstep sandwiches. Fortunately, the ingredients of each sandwich overcame the crude method of construction that encased it.

By the time I had finished eating, the ponies had largely dispersed. Some, including mother and foal, were still visible close to the horizon. Just.

We continued to traverse that part of the moor. Then we headed back in the mid-afternoon. Once again, I noticed his tendency to veer towards the Great Mire as we passed it. But he stayed with me to the crossroads before turning back to the moor. True to form!

The following morning to my relief there he was, dutifully stationed on the mound next to the mire.

We set off with him evincing far less interest in the mire itself. He was going lickety-split ahead of me and I was pedalling furiously. The weather was glorious and all seemed well until …

Tikka casually turned his head. Turned it the once towards the Great Mire now only just visible. That single glance changed everything as he came to a halt. His ears flattened. His top lip rose to reveal his fangs. He seemed transfixed, yet his eyes blazed with fury.

I crunched to a stop on the wiry heather. "Whatever is it, boy? What have you seen?"

I might as well not have been present. A low menacing growl escaped those bared fangs. This first sound I had ever heard from him seemed to come down a long, echoing tunnel. It was directed at something on the mire's edge – a dark, shapeless mass.

Grabbing my bird-watching field glasses, I trained them on that exact spot. Then my trembling fingers fumbled with their focus mechanism. What I finally saw will stay with me until the close of my own earthly existence! Even today the memory of it converts my blood to ice-water!

Chapter Seven

"There was a fing – sorry, thing – Mr P. Beside the Great Mire. All dark and shadowy-like. I'm telling the truth – honest injun!"

The next morning, I had sought out the one adult likely to believe me. There should be more adults like Mr Pargeter – Mr P – on his log! He fixed me with his wonky eye and smiled grimly.

"I know when a lad is telling it like it is. Don't you fret."

"It came out of a sort of black cloud. A sort of man-thing, with an enormous belly. Sort of all wrapped round."

"Too many pies. No, I'm just teasing you, boy. How come you know he was fat if he was all wrapped round? Do you mean wrapped in a cloak? No more 'sort ofs' please."

"Yeah, a cloak-thing. Even so, his great belly was poking through."

"OK. You saw a shadow-man step from a kind of earth cloud. Then what?"

"He turned slowly towards us. Lucky we were so far away. Through my bird glasses I could see his eyes. The rest of his face was shadowy, but his eyes seemed to burn like … like …"

"Twin fires?"

"Yeah! He looked like some demon. I had to lower my binocs. He turned my tummy."

"I should think so."

"Do demons exist, Mr P? In one of my 10d comics there is this geezer – Captain Lightfoot. He fights them. Only they ain't so dark and shadowy as this one. I think that cloud must have been soot – or something. Is it a demon, Mr P?"

"No demon. They exist all right, but what you saw was likely him."

"Him?"

The old man's eyes looked far-away. He was retreating into memory. "My grandpa understood spooky stuff. I can tell tales and legends but he was one for the spooks, was Grandpa. The Golden Path. He spoke often of the Golden Path."

"What's that when it's at home?"

"Something that can only be seen by those with the Inner Eye. He had the Inner Eye and so do you, lad. Something to be proud of. It's how you see old Whatsit … er, Ticker. Sounds like my heart."

"What is this Gold Path thing, Mr P?"

"All 'thing' with you! Not thing! Not gold. Golden Path!!" He seemed awestruck by his own words. "When spirits don't – or can't – go to their eternal rest 'cus of some shock, or death was all too sudden for 'em like, they roams their own locality or the scene of anything that troubled them in life. Like your old Ticker does."

"Tikka! So, where's this Golden Path come in?"

"The Supreme Intelligence behind the universe …"

"God?"

"The Supreme Intelligence is clued in – or so Grandpa told me – to when the good spirits have finally fully adjusted to what has happened. He sends down the Golden Path to fetch 'em up."

"Fetch 'em up to where?"

"Obvious! Paradise. Heaven. What the Vikings called Valhalla! A better place than this. Their reward for being good against all the pressures in this old world to be otherwise."

"Will Tikka get to go, on this Golden Path – thing? Sorry."

"Course. A good and faithful hound. I reckon his master and mistress come out of the mire and roam a bit late at night. Maybe a bit earlier and longer on them two evenings you say he didn't turn up. Probably keeping near them, what with 'him' about."

"Him again. Who is this sooty geezer? I thought demon, like in my comic. Then I thought Death. Is Death a person?"

"Angel of Death, you mean? Like in the Good Book. Spot any wings? Nah, he ain't carrying off first-born, this one. Nah. Him is the one she ran through with the spike. Remember? What she did was wrong but he is pure evil. Spirits finally go in one of two directions – up or down. Harp or shovel. Only one thing can delay evil spirits getting on the down slope. The thirst for revenge. Vengeance can cause an evil spirit to linger. Outstay their welcome for centuries. He is still around, boy."

"What does he want to do by way of revenge? How do you know it's him?"

"Don't need to be Hercules Parrot."

"Who?"

"The cloak boy. He ain't fat. It's covering the spike. It's still in him."

"Wow! Can he harm my Tikka?"

"It's her he's after. But he'll take on the whole package to get to her. The hunter again. Her of course, and Tikka – yes."

"How will he …?"

"By stepping into the Golden Path. My guess is the time of the Golden Path is near. Very near!! That's why that evil one is showing himself and the hunter and the maiden are more restless."

"Does Tikka know that?"

"He'll be sensing it, boy. He'll want to go with them."

"So what does it matter if this sooty guy steps into the Golden Path?"

"Matter? It would be contaminated! The hunter, the hunter's gal and Tikka – if he can hitch the ride – will be slung out of the Golden Path. It stretches from heaven to earth, you see. According to Grandpa when evil enters it the path is withdrawn immediately to be…er…leansed of any rottenness that's intruded."

"So what happens to the good spirits once they are slung out?"

"They falls back to earth. Unharmed, but they may have to linger century at least to get another crack at the Golden Path. As to the evil one, he will go straight to the lake of fire you saw reflected in his eyes. Revenge will be a poor consolation for that tormenting place."

"So I'm going to lose Tikka if this evil thing – sorry, evil spirit – fails somehow to gum up the works."

"'Fraid you must be prepared to let Ticker go when the time comes. My guess is he's keeping his eye on the mire knowing that his master and mistress are down there, when they are not roaming. Down there, waiting for the Golden Path. It only comes at night and I'll bet he'll try and stop that evil one from hopping on board and ruining their chances to leave the mire."

"Do spirits fight, then?"

"Yep, according to Grandpa. I only hope that your Ticker does not lose his chance to go with his old master and mistress. It would fair break his ghost-heart to have to wait long, long years for another chance without 'em being around."

"I see." My eyes misted a little and Mr P patted my hand in his kindly fashion. "Can this evil spirit kill my Tikka? Can ghost or spirits, whatever, die a second death?"

"All I know is they can fight! The outcome is beyond my knowledge and I suspect Grandpa's, 'cus he never mentioned it. Like I say, when the time of the Golden Path does come, let's just hope your Ticker is not so busy fighting the evil one he loses his own chance to go with those he loves most."

He paused and delved into his jacket pocket. Out with the usual debris came the little carving.

"Here, this is yours."

"But it's so precious to you, Mr P. I can't …"

"Can and will. Bless you, boy. It should belong to somebody with the Inner Eye and I don't qualify. I have only a single good outer eye. As far as it stretches it can only pick up on one person, worthy to receive this carving. A little 'n famous for overuse of the word 'thing', but definitely equipped with inside vision."

"I don't know what to say."

"There's a first! I might leave that mouth-cosy off my Christmas list! One last thing – now I'm at it, saying thing!"

"Yes?"

"Stay away from that mire. There is grave danger there. You are just an iddy biddy lad! Leave it to your old Ticker mate to sort things! Savvy?"

"Yes."

Chapter Eight

The summer holidays were over. Tikka and I were back to our old routine of meeting at the crossroads each evening. I was so relieved to find him there.

What did he know? If Mr Pargeter was to be believed, we were on borrowed time – or our relationship was!

My other relationship – with Sal – was slipping. She was inclining more towards Fearless Freddy. True, he thought nature was something in the way when he was playing football. But he paid her lots of attention and even bought her little presents out of his pocket money. His allowance was more generous than mine, so it was no contest.

If I tried to visit Sal with invisible Tikka in tow he simply turned back towards the moor. So the little twilight conferences Sal and I were used to having on her porch became infrequent.

At weekends I cycled on the moor but I did not encounter my ghost-dog any more during the full daylight hours. No, not even when I went as near the Great Mire as I dared with that 'thing' somewhere around.

Then it happened! The sun was just going off-duty and the moon was struggling to make its presence felt through a tattered cloud bank. A chilly evening with a hint of coming winter. I had been freewheeling down a favourite slope on the edge of the moor. Normally, Tikka would study my every move, but this time he seemed restless and distracted.

I always honoured my promise to Mum to be home by 7:45 pm. Partly out of respectful regard, partly not to lose my evening freedom privileges. Even more so since Mum had only just begun to thaw out after Aunt Millie's tantrums. Disobedience was not an option if I wanted to live!

Aunt Millie apparently had made a lightning recovery. This was aided by an unexpected visit from a lonely widower (and fellow housey-housey type) who had just scooped the jackpot. He wanted her to accompany him on a few seaside outings. All expenses paid!

Aunt Millie, all soft and fluttery, took to make-up and false eyelashes. Mum was shown the door. The extent of Aunt Millie's gratitude for weeks of nursing was underwhelming. No, it wouldn't do to upset Mum now.

So I turned my bike towards the crossroads. I anticipated that Tikka would follow as usual. We always said goodbye there.

Instead, he suddenly turned and headed across the moor. There was an urgency about him as he went. Something inside me told me this was it!! To use modern parlance – it was 'game-time, baby'!!! To my shame, I followed.

I was able to keep up. Well, just! Tikka stayed within the beam of my bike lights, obligingly enough, but he was starting to accelerate. His powerful limbs flowed so gracefully but purposefully with that mounting urgency.

We were nearing the Great Mire and he wasn't stopping. I don't know whether I was going bonkers – or more than slightly brave. Neither characteristic belonged with me. Well, not in my own estimation.

My heart was like a hammer crashing on an anvil. Then suddenly we were on the edge of the mire. I dismounted, switching off my bike lights as Tikka vanished in the gloom ahead of me. I seized my super-powerful flashlight from my saddlebag and leaned the bike against some bushes. The flashlight had been a present from an ex-military uncle.

Then I thought to myself, What the heck – *the more light the better.* I switched the bike lights back on so my trusty chariot would be easier to locate later. It was not exactly the Blackpool illuminations but if the thing wanted to locate me.

If your estimation of me comes down heavily on the side of temporary insanity you might be right. But remember how fond I was of my ghost-dog. Think of what any one of you kids would do for your own live pooch. So nothing would have stopped me following Tikka into that mire.

The cloud-enfeebled moon tried to help out with lighting my path. But as I began to follow Tikka something very odd was occurring around me. True, I had never entered the Great Mire before. But I had been up to the margins of it. What I had seen was rough grassy and bushy 'safe' areas intersected by swampy, marshy bits laden with menace.

However, the flashlight revealed that the 'safe' areas were much more waterlogged than I remembered. Also, the swampy bits seemed even more frequent and threatening. Dark, sinister patches to the right and left of me! My shoes squelched on paths hard to separate from those grim dark patches.

With water leaking uncomfortably into my socks I persisted. Fear was attacking me on two fronts. One – fear of being sucked down due to one careless step. Two – fear that 'the thing' would find me.

It found me all right!

Chapter Nine

Suddenly Tikka passed from my sight. Although I blessed my military flashlight and prayed it would not fail me, I felt so vulnerable. So alone!

The paths – for want of a better word – were becoming squelchier and squelchier. This was definitely not the Great Mire I had previously eyeballed from safe vantage points on the moor. No, my little friends, it wasn't! This was a step back in time! This was worthy of Dr Who, to use modern parlance again.

Horrified at this realisation, I heard a long, unearthly, echoing howl ahead of me. Hounds of the Baskervilles stuff! I think even Sherlock Holmes would have turned back, but that howl could only have come from my Tikka.

In a moment I found myself on the bushy, shrubby lip of a slope. I almost tumbled down it. I steadied myself and pointed the flashlight down the incline. At the base was a gully. On its broad floor was a sinister, almost treacly mass. Swamp!! Uugh! It seemed almost alive. Organic. Yuk!

At the side of it was a rocky, shingly area. Lying on it, staring into the Quatermassy thing was my Tikka. Right next to him, protruding from a softer patch of earth was what looked like the shaft of a spear. Was this the same decorated spear that belonged to the huntsman all those centuries ago? I gasped. How could it still … Of course! Time warp! I was in a time warp! I had heard the phrase on my favourite radio programme *Journey Into Space*. Jet Morgan, the hero astronaut, said to his space engineer, "Lemmy, we are in a time warp". Well, so was I. So was Tikka.

The slope was too steep to slither down. Besides, I did not want to lose my precious flashlight – or damage it. It was my lifeline. Cautiously, I worked my way along the edge of the slope, consigning Tikka back to the semi-light afforded by the cloud-plagued moon. That shingly, rocky bit, which was like what's left when a river tide goes out, suddenly vanished. Petered out. There was only the swamp below like some greedy, devouring monster about to be roused from slumber.

I turned back. Rather, I started to turn. 'The thing' found me!!

I was aware of a dark, icy force that seemed to engulf me. My precious flashlight mercifully fell into a bush, but its light was enfeebled by the shadow of 'the thing'. No way could I turn fully. Nor did I want to. But I fought and struggled to free myself from the ice-cold iron grip of 'the thing'. Fought and struggled as never before. As never since!

Fortunately, when I started to turn, I was a few feet from the rim of the slope. I say fortunately, for it was clear to me 'the thing' was heaving me to the slope edge in order to precipitated me into that revolting mass below.

I could see the red glow from its ghastly eyes reflected on the narrow strip of ground between me and a plunge to certain death. No way was I going to look into those eyes at close range, but I could see its ebony arms enclosing my body. See and feel them! Solid and icy!

In my blind, threshing panic I somehow remembered the spike that still penetrated 'the thing's body'. I managed to make contact with projecting wood and bump it up and down. I felt 'the thing' recoil and even loosen its hold. Yes, it could feel pain all right!

Remembering something my military uncle had taught me, I tried to become a dead weight, falling back off my feet, now on the slope rim. I might as well have been a feather, and I found myself looking into the swamp with seconds to spare. Seconds to live!

Panic-stricken, I reached backwards with both hands. I yanked desperately on the spike projection. 'The thing' swirled its dark force around me and emitted a dreadful, hollow shriek. Pain or rage – or both. But for the second time its grip loosened and I was able to snake back slightly from the slope edge, buying oh-so-precious moments!

'The thing', however, seemed suddenly renewed. My hands were ripped loose from the spike. My poor, aching arms were forced agonisingly up my back by that icy grip of steel. At the same time the push towards and over the rim of the slope began again.

In my mind I was saying goodbye to Mum, Dad, Sal, Fearless Freddy – even Morton – and of course Tikka. I even asked Scruffy Hollershaw to forgive me for turning his baggy underpants into a playground display. How I managed to crowd so much thought into so little time I will never know. But the dominant thought was that it was all up with me!

The thing's eyes were generating quite a heat in contrast to its ice-cold limbs. That heat was mounting. I felt I was either going to burn up or freeze before I was dropped into the ominous gully below.

Then it happened! Out of nowhere came Tikka my ghost-dog as I had never seen him before! Fangs bared, eyes that reflected that hideous red glow from the thing's own eyes. He looked more like a dog-demon. Awesome!!

Snarling, enraged, he flung himself onto the dark mass behind me. I remembered Mr Pargeter's words about spirits fighting each other.

To my total relief, I felt released from the vice-like grip behind my back. Sobbing with pain in my arms, I lowered them as the dark, red-eyed mass moved to one side. Breathing like some express steam train, I lay on the lip of the slope with no fight left in me. I was dimly aware of the titanic struggle beside me.

When I managed to lift my gaze, I glimpsed briefly the bulk of a man in the sooty, inky haze that surrounded him. It was trying to free himself from the fangs of my Tikka fastened on his throat. Even more fearsome was the fact that Tikka's hind legs were balancing on the spike-shaft. I looked away so as not to catch that red-eyed, luminous stare of 'the thing', now writhing and screaming hollowly, clearly in agony from the pressure on the spike.

Then it happened! The entire dark mass with Tikka – my Tikka – at its heart overbalanced and plunged down the slope into the swamp below, fighting, struggling all the while, even as the twosome sank from sight in that treacly gunge.

"Tikka! Tikka!" I sobbed. "Come back! Come back!!"

Silence, deep as the ocean, was all that greeted me!

Chapter Ten

Panting and sobbing, I seized my flashlight. Still functioning, thank God.

The beam picked out the slope's treacherous margin as I made my way cautiously along it. Then, as I reached the point where the spear still projected from the shingle below …

I honestly thought the moon had escaped its cloudy tormentors. But no! As I lifted my gaze, I saw a wondrous sight indeed!

In the cloudy but star-pricked heavens, another light was appearing. Like the moon beside it, this light was well above those scattered cloud levels. Unlike the moon, its beams were unobstructed. Also, it was growing in intensity into a mellow, beautiful, golden radiance.

It enabled me to switch off my flashlight. I stared up into it, fascinated, entranced, bewitched. It's hard to explain, kids, but I had a feeling like I wanted to be absorbed into that light – become part of it. It was as if all the horror I had just experienced was melting away as I gazed at it.

"What are you?" I breathed. "Are you anything to do with the Golden Path?"

As if answering me, the beams came together. Consolidated into a broad, winding, serpentine, golden pathway, stretching from heaven to earth! Unbelievable!

The beams just fell short of me but bathed the gully slopes and the swamp below. Where it caught the shingly 'beach', I could see that the spear-shaft was ornamented with crude little carvings. Perhaps they were carved by the same hand that shaped my little man/dog statuette – the huntsman's hands?

As the dancing beams engulfed the spear handle, the whole thing lifted. The buried spear tip was revealed, dislodged from its soil host. The spear also began to dance within the Golden Path ascending until it was several feet above the ground, turning inwards. Then suddenly, it was stillish and vertical with the tapered part pointing downwards.

I had a stupid impulse I should perhaps have resisted. For some unaccountable reason, I had brought along in my pocket the miniature carving given to me by Mr Pargeter. Why, I'll never know, but I flung it with all my remaining strength into the Golden Path. The outer beams embraced it, pulling it into a glowing central core.

Like the spear, it bobbed and weaved a while. Then it came to rest alongside the spear, both floating gently on those waves of luminosity at the pathway's heart.

Next came the most wonderful thing of all! A fissure began to open up on the swamp surface, widening, widening, until … at the base of the Golden Path, where its core touched the swamp, a man's head, crowned with unruly hair, emerged from the treacly mass A powerful head followed by a bull-neck, as we used to term it. A thick neck like a circus strongman's, enclosed by a hairy collar that looked half chewed away.

Gradually, the powerful shoulders and torso emerged and finally the whole man with legs like miniature tree trunks. He was all encased in furs but the power and strength of him was visibly abnormal. He made today's Arnie Schwarzenegger look like a wimp!!!

Yet big and heavy as he was, he rose into the Golden Path and bobbed about on those light-waves just like the spear and the little carving. He seemed light as a feather as he came to a fixed position beside them.

As he floated there the fissure seemed to open even further. Out of it came a woman, very strongly built, in a robe that covered her from her shoulders to just above her sandaled feet. Her long fair tresses of hair drifted on the light-waves that swept her upwards until he was level with the man. They embraced each other with their strongly muscled arms.

I noted that all the gunge of the swamp, so evident as they emerged, had fallen back to earth. They were left clean and pure, looking like two angels – only with muscles!

The base of the Golden Path began to rise but the two persons stayed above that with barely a movement. It was as if the whole thing was being hauled up by an invisible hand somewhere in the heavens. The light above was now too blinding for me to see.

My thoughts turned hysterically to Tikka. *Had he lost his battle with that terrible thing? Had they both suffered some kind of second death? Were they still fighting it out below the swamp surface?*

The fissure began to close. I called out in total desperation.

"Tikka! Tikka! Where are you? You will miss your chance!"

A tiny piece of me that was resisting losing him suddenly surrendered. Something within me accepted that it was time to let go of him. Feeling-wise, I mean.

Whether there was any connection I do not know, but in that same moment of my acceptance he appeared. My Tikka! Sorry – our Tikka! A long-muzzled head burst out of the narrowing fissure and his furry bulk struggled onto the surface of the swamp. Not a moment too soon as the gap closed beneath him!

The mud and gunge seemed to fall away, leaving him looking resplendent – more beautiful than I had seen him before. He looked up at the Golden Path. The base of it was several feet above him but I knew he could see his master and mistress encased within it.

The ground beneath him looked suddenly, unaccountably solid. I wanted him to look my way but his tense body signalled his intention. All his focus was on that retreating stream of gold light. It was the leap of leaps! Beyond any earthly canine. The jump of jumps!!

"Go on, boy!" My voice was hoarse – cracked with emotion. I held out no hope of him bridging that immense gap – especially upwards. But what an effort!

To my amazement his head and shoulders and forelegs penetrated the base of the Golden Path. But the rest of his body dangled on the night air. Whatever would become of him now? Would he fall back to earth and lose his chance to go to 'Valhalla' after winning his battle with 'the thing'.

I could see his forepaws scrabbling in vain to maintain a purchase on that straightening, luminous trail. But he was slipping inexorably downwards. His fate seemed inevitable. It was so horribly unfair after he had saved me and ensured the purity of the Golden Path by eliminating 'the thing'. How could any power of good – Mr Pargeter's 'Intelligent mind behind the Universe' – allow him to lose his chance of going with his beloved first master and mistress?

I had reckoned without that intelligent mind and its goodness. At the umpteenth moment as Tikka's shoulders were nearly level with the pathway's base, I saw the man begin to work his way down the tunnel of gold, almost like he was swimming. He hooked his powerful sandaled feet round Tikka's head and drew his mighty legs up towards his stomach. Tikka was pulled up and onto the core of the Golden Path where I could see his tail vibrating and swirling the beams of light like the fizz in some gold mineral water.

Soon the light trail was far above and its trio had diminished to mere specks within it. Finally, it was absorbed into the massive luminescence above the clouds – and even above the moon itself, now floating free and clear. That gold light lingered a moment, then dissipated into a faint yellow vapour rivalling the clouds. Then nothing. Just the night and me.

"Goodbye Tikka," I muttered. "Thanks for being my friend. I shall miss you for ever and ever. Amen."

Mum always made me say The Lord's Prayer. I still do. Last thing every night. Right then, its final words seemed especially appropriate!

I picked up my flashlight, still functioning though I kicked it several times in my struggle with 'the thing'.

Mysteriously, when I shone my flashlight on my clothes there was no visible sign of that frantic struggle with 'the thing'! Not a tear, nor a tatter. Not a speck of mud – or even 'squelch' on my shoes and socks. *How do you account for that?*

Most of my fears had evaporated like the Golden Path itself. One at least remained. Facing parental wrath at my being out so long and late.

The situation also worked out in my favour. I located my bike and pedalled furiously homeward only to find that I had not been missed. There was nobody to miss me!

Under the usual porch flowerpot an explanatory note in Mum's familiar biro-scrawl kept company with the spare front door key. It seemed that Aunt Millie had suffered a so-called relapse. She felt it her duty to summon poor Mum to her bedside. We later worked out that her relapse coincided with the discovery that her widower friend had run through his jackpot money.

Since Dad was working overtime at the timber yard, that only left Morton to note my late coming. He was no grass! Too busy consuming the stuff, alternating it with his precious salt tablet. What is it with guinea pigs and salt?

Anyway, I marvelled at how things had worked out. Everything was going like clockwork now.

If I thought that was the end of matters, I reckoned without that 'Intelligent Mind' behind the universe. It had one final card to play!

Postscript

The years have come and gone, kids. Difficult to explain but somehow I outgrew my little moorland village.

You see, when I left school I worked briefly in an office in town. Hated it! Bored stiff! Perhaps that is why I was lured into the army by a television recruiting film. It assured me – in grainy black and white – that army life was all sports and recreation. Climbing, hiking etc. It wasn't!!

Dad's delight was based on his limited experience of something called National Service. Mum was more tight-lipped. After a few years of military life, I mentally awarded the prize to Mum!

Two foreign wars fulfilled the clichéd promise contained in the recruiting film. They 'made a man of me'. *At what cost, though?*

Kids, don't let anyone fool you there is glory in war. Heroism, yes. Comradeship, yes. But war wears a mask. Strip it off and the face beneath is ugly and bloody. The innocent and defenceless suffer most. If you do decide to join up as adults, do it to protect them and bring them peace and security.

However, my army experience proved invaluable in one way. It gave me a plum job! After I was demobbed (discharged) I became something called – very grandly – a security consultant.

My somewhat over-generous salary enabled me to occupy a luxury apartment overlooking the Thames. I am there to this day.

Somehow, with my army experiences and the passage of time, I lost touch in my mind with that eeriest of childhood experiences. Concerning Tikka, I mean! I even managed to con myself that it was just a boyhood fantasy.

Occasionally, I would return to the village to visit my parents. But I no longer belonged. War had changed me. A fish out of water, as we used to say. The only person I could converse with comfortably was Fearless Freddy's ex-paratrooper Dad who had also seen terrible things.

Death comes to us all. Dad passed away very peacefully and Mum followed quite shortly – of a broken heart. Yes, there is such a thing! They had been devoted to each other.

Mum willed me the house. I had no use for it and sold it on cheaply to Fearless Freddy and Super-Sal – now an item. It would enable them to shift from their shoddy village cottage with its dated plumbing.

Before they moved in, I paid the house a final visit. Just a couple of days and nights. I don't know why. Sentimental reasons perhaps.

On the second evening, I took a stroll down to the crossroads in the twilight. A strange sadness gripped me. It worsened as I passed the late Mr Pargeter's cottage, now occupied by his niece. The log was still in place, but crumbling and rotting now under a greenish mould.

I knew that kindly Mr P was destined for a harp, not a shovel. *Was he already plucking that harp astride some far-off cloud? Or was his spirit nearby?* Lurking and waiting for its turn to ascend to … wherever … on the Golden Path. I was shocked that my mind had thrown up such boyhood notions. I thought I had outgrown them, but no ... Perhaps it was the sight of the log in the twilight that had re-hooked me.

On my infrequent visits to my parents over the years, I seldom allowed myself to linger at the crossroads. Mostly I would try to time myself to catch the town bus. Tonight, I lingered!

The wind rose. It flapped my coat. The moon added its mellow glow to the newish single street light creating long shadows on the road surface. A bat skimmed me.

Suddenly, I found myself reliving the whole Tikka business. All that had happened since seemed to fade away. My heart ached for my ghost-dog of long ago.

In that moment I began to sense something. A presence perhaps? Was that a slight flurry of movement beyond the corner of my right eye? Then the left? Something just keeping out of my vision no matter how quickly I turned my head.

"Tikka." I breathed. "Is it you?"

Nothing!

Even so, as I walked back to the house there was again this sense of a presence. Something – or someone rather – walking with me, unseen.

It had hurt me when Tikka, concentrating on his mighty leap from the swamp to the Golden Path, had failed to acknowledge me or even glance in my direction. Of course, he was totally poised and focused. Had to be! But that had not taken away a nagging doubt from my mind. *Had I meant anything to him at all?*

As I entered the house, something obstructed me from closing the front door. Only briefly, but I felt a pressure on the lower part, between door and frame. Had something entered behind me? Something about dog height?

Nervous about this possible presence, I switched on all the downstairs lights quickly.

Sal and Freddy had asked to retain much of the old household furniture. Even under 60-watt bulbs it all looked eerie and ghostly with its covering of dust sheets. I elected to steady my nerves by brewing a cuppa in the kitchen. Standard British remedy for the collywobbles!

Mum's aged kettle sang out its boiling point from the stove. Simultaneously, I heard a distinct scuffling sound in the hallway.

I steeled myself to investigate, reminding me that I was an old soldier. That reminder just about forced me out through the kitchen doorway. A strong draught assaulted me. My astonished gaze registered that the front door was now wide open.

Had I not closed it firmly behind ... whatever? Did this mean that the presence had somehow managed to reopen it and leave by the way it had come in?

I closed the front door again. Then I carried my mug of tea into the living room. I almost dropped the mug. As I entered, my eye fell on an object clearly visible on the well-worn carpet. An object I thought I would never see again.

It was that tiny wooden statuette of a huntsman and his dog!

END